The Snow Queen

Illustrated by Alan Marks

Retold by Lesley Sims
Based on a story by Hans Christian Andersen

Edited by Jenny Tyler
Designed by Andrea Slane
Cover design by Russell Punter

Long, long ago,

and even further away,

lived two best friends, Gerda and Kay.

In all the world, no two friends were as close.

One crisp winter's day, Kay was crunching through the snow
when he saw a twinkling snowflake.

It grew larger...

and larger...

until, suddenly, it turned
into a woman, dressed in
a sparkling white cloak.

The next second, she was gone.

The following afternoon, Kay was with Gerda when - ow! - a sharp speck of ice flew into his eye. From that moment, everything changed.

Kay began teasing Gerda and ripping up all her precious flowers. Then he made fun of people in the street.

As each day passed, he grew more and more horrible.

"Whatever's happened to Kay?" Gerda asked her grandmother.
Gerda's grandmother shook her head sadly and sighed.
"I think he's been enchanted by the Snow Queen," she said.

After a while, Kay ignored Gerda altogether. He only wanted to play outside in the snow.

His cheeks glowed and his eyes shone.

He never seemed to notice the cold.

On the coldest day of the winter, the Snow Queen came for Kay.
In a daze, he caught hold of her sleigh.

She commanded her snow-white horse
in a voice spikier than icicles.

HOME!

And they flew from the market square, Kay clinging on behind.

The Snow Queen took Kay far, far away, to her palace of ice in the frozen north.

Kay grew colder, and colder, and colder...
so cold, he might have been carved from ice himself.

Week after week, he sat still as a snowman,
trapped in a room made from blocks of ice.

Soon, he completely forgot Gerda and everything in his old life.

But Gerda didn't forget Kay.

As the flowers started to bloom,
she set off to look for him.

First, she followed
the winding river.

When the river ran out, she left her boat and walked.
She walked for days and days...

...until, lost and alone in a forest, she finally stopped. A glossy black crow hopped up to her. "Caaaaw," he croaked. "What's wrong?"

"I'm looking for my friend," she said. "The Snow Queen stole him." "A queen?" croaked the crow. "Perhaps she's taken him to the palace by the lake. Caaaaaaw. I'll show you."

He led Gerda through sleeping halls,
where royal dreams glided past.
"Try the robbers' castle," they
whispered. "Take the golden
coach outside."

The robbers' castle stood high on a hill, stark against the sky.

Following a moonlit path, the golden coach rattled its way to the top.

Inside the castle, Gerda told her story again.

"The Snow Queen lives in the frozen north,"
said a robber girl. "My reindeer can take you."

The robber girl watched them go, waving until Gerda and her reindeer were out of sight.

They had a long, hard journey ahead.

The air turned cold and stung Gerda's face like hail.
Her face went numb but still they kept going.

At last, towering in the distance, she saw the Snow Queen's
glittering palace of ice.

In a whirl of snowflakes, the Queen's guards sprang at Gerda.

As Gerda cried out,
her breath formed
into misty angels.

Silently, they
swooped down and
attacked the palace guards.

Gerda ran into the palace calling for Kay.

She put her hand over his frozen
heart and it began to thaw.
A warm tear melted the speck of
ice in Kay's eye and trickled down
his cheek. "Gerda?" he whispered.

Kay jumped up, sending blocks of ice flying.
The Snow Queen could only watch in
icy fury, as Gerda and Kay fled, leaving her
chilly palace forever.

Back at home, Gerda's grandmother was overjoyed to see them. "I can't believe you escaped the Snow Queen!" she cried, over and over again.

And she hugged them both tightly, as if she'd never, ever let them go.